MW00904044

The Snow Family: Viola Player Found

Also by Kevin Elkington

Sixth Grade and Growing Up

Green Family: New Home

Seventh Grade and Friendship

The Green Family: Grateful

Eighth Grade and Togetherness

The Green Family: Blessings

The Hsu Family: Finding Happiness

The Green Family: Bailey Being Bailey

The Hsu Family: Calvin and Pedro, Good Friends

The Green Family: Brandon's Tree

The Hsu Family: Emma and Her Cat

The Green Family: Little Things in Life

The Snow Family: A Place Called Home

The Snow Family: Viola Player Found

By

Kevin Elkington

For my loving parents, who inspired me to write books.

This is a work of fiction. Names, characters, places, and incidents either are the product of the author's imagination or are used fictitiously. Any resemblance to actual persons, living or dead, events, or locales is entirely coincidental.

Copyright © 2020 Kevin Elkington

All rights reserved.

ISBN: 9781657807334

I am grateful for the support of my parents, who inspired me to start writing books.

Greetings from Forest Falls, Wisconsin.

Have a happy day from the Rose Café!

Thank you very much for inviting my book into your home in order for my book to be read.

Table of Contents

CHAPTER ONE

PEP TALK

One Saturday after our family breakfast, George, Brandon, Emily, and Mom were still sitting at the kitchen nook table.

Mom wanted to have a little chat with us all. Mom took a sip of her coffee, and looked at me, Brandon, George, my older brother, and Emily, my little sister. She told us that "We, the Snow family, have been living lives of privilege. Do not walk away when someone needs help."

Mom continued, "We also need to continue to pay attention to how we live."

Paying attention to how we live, our mother always emphasizes to us – George, Brandon, and Emily – that we need to be good students at school and that we need to make something of ourselves.

What do you want out of your life?

An even more challenging questions is: what is it that consumes your thoughts, time, and energy?

She always reminded us that we live in two worlds: this earthly one and a heavenly one. When we are blinded by our own personal satisfaction, it is easy to become lukewarm about our personal inner spiritual matters. You lose your perspective in life and you end up losing what is correct.

Setting your hearts on the lesser things of this world not only robs us of heavenly treasure, it also keeps us from enjoying the spiritual blessings.

Sometime later, Emily asked Brandon, "What was Mom saying, when she said, do not walk away when someone needs help?"

Brandon told Emily, "What Mom is telling us is that when someone falls, help them stand up. Always hold the door for another person and always say thank you. In another words, be kind to people."

"I knew you could explain it to me a lot better than George did," Emily said as she continued to talk.

"No wonder why Masato always tells me that you are super smart, cute, and someone who plays piano awesomely."

CHAPTER TWO

BRANDON

On the bus the second day of sixth grade, I, Brandon, decided to head straight to the back. But, halfway down the aisle, Masato from my math class looked up from the book she was reading.

"Brandon, here," as she patted the seat next to her as she scooted toward the window.

Since Masato's Dad is my piano teacher, I decided the better part of being cool was just acting cool. So I smiled and sat next to her.

"Hi," she said, "I'm Masato, from math class," she said jokingly.

I nodded, "I know." Brandon laughed.

Masato smiled, "Thanks for sitting next to me on the bus. All last year, the seat next to me was empty, and it was very strange and awkward. I thought it stinks at first – but now I have a bus sitting buddy."

I grinned, and said, "Thanks," to Masato.

Masato put her book she was reading inside her book bag and started talking. "I have heard about your experience yesterday finding the science lab class. You don't need to worry, no one really pays attention to those popular stuck up students. There are nice students in the grade too. I will introduce you to them."

"Cool! Fantastic!" Brandon said. Masato and I chatted the rest of the way to school. Masato, like me, plays a classical instrument. She also loves to read and write. Her favorite subject is English and she loves to play the *violin*.

I, Brandon, love to play classical piano music and I love to read Louis L'Amour books. My favorite subjects are science and math, while Masato's favorite subjects are not those ones.

Both of us agreed that the school librarian, Mrs. September, is a little quirky. She is very unique, smart, and is a very nice and interesting teacher. She is a teacher as well.

As the bus pulled in, Masato and I, Brandon, shuffled off and Masato said, "I will see you in math class!"

At that moment, I knew that after having known Masato for over two years, I was lucky to have my fabulous, fantastic, good friend Masato at Jefferson Middle School.

CHAPTER THREE

FIRST SNOW AND LAST SNOW

Yes, the first snow has finally arrived. That was over two years ago – when the Snow family first moved to Forest Falls, Wisconsin.

My cute – sweet – little sister, Emily, had been very much looking forward to seeing her very first white snow. When she found out the snow was coming, I do not think Emily slept at all.

It was all the excitement that she caused when the white floppy snow finally fell. You just could not believe all the commotion and running around and screaming that she caused. All this over something such as the first coming of snow.

Now looking back after two years of living in Forest Falls, Wisconsin, after two winters of snow storms; Emily is over it with regards to the new-bee-ness of white snow. That means that snowing is not a big deal!

Believe it or not – now she is looking forward to our last snow storm of the upcoming year.

CHAPTER FOUR

FINDING GOOD FRIENDS IS NOT EASY

Looking back:

Yes, my mother was right about one thing, my new school was absolutely – fabulous, super – beautiful.

I couldn't help admiring all the swooping open spaces and comfy lounges, skylights, terraces with seating, and the green plants everywhere.

I had to admit that Jefferson Middle School was way nicer than my old school in Pleasant Valley, California.

The only problem was that it was really difficult to navigate around.

The hallway – there were no straight hallways! I tried walking one way, and the room numbers went in the opposite direction.

I tried walking the other way, but those rooms had letters and not numbers on them.

I was going to be late!

I clutched the corners of the hallway – then I was intently studying my next class location, and then I was studying the map hoping someone would pass by me and offer to help.

That is what I thought, anyway.

Hey, are you lost?

I looked up – this girl was looking at me curiously but not meanly. I thought that to myself. Maybe this was good, maybe this was one of those things where the girls were nice when they were apart but not so nice when they were together.

Anyway, I took a deep breath and said, "Do you know how to get to the science lab class, room C 342, by any chance?"

She grinned widely and said, "Sure! It's easy, head down to the lower basement, and it's right past the atrium on your right! You can't miss it." I, Brandon, said, "Okay, thanks a lot!" I saw her off, and I set off down the stairs in relief. I was just pulling open the door when all I saw were rows of desks with computers.

I then heard a very stern voice. "Are you meant to be in this class, young man?"

I turned quickly and found myself face-to-face with a small, quirky, middle-aged woman with a lot of salt than pepper hair, with red-around-the-rim glasses perched on her nose.

She was dressed in a red coat and a red dress with a wide leather belt.

I was very much confused and did not know what to do – how – or – I started to stammer, holding the map out toward her. "I'm lost," I said clearly.

Her expression softened, "Oh, you are new. Where are you supposed to be?"

Let's see, I thought. Without thinking I held out the schedule to her.

"You are way off; the science labs are all the way on the third floor – how on earth did you end up down here in the basement?" She sighed heavily.

"I had better take you up in the elevator." She began walking very briskly up the hall. She is used to walking and talking a mile a minute.

"I'm Mrs. September. I'm the librarian." Brandon was thinking to himself - that was the library – he remembered the lowest level contains the library and all of the English classrooms.

Mrs. September was talking, saying: reading is very pivotal and important here at Jefferson Middle School - all students must have an independent reading book at all times. Therefore, you gain knowledge and be smart!

"If you ever need or if you don't have a book, always come see me...." said Mrs. September.

Mrs. September and I hopped into the elevator, and she continued her chatter. I really did not know, or try to answer what seemed like a question, but it was as if Mrs. September didn't really need the answer.

Therefore, I just kept listening as she kept on talking.

The elevator pinged when it got to the third floor and the doors opened.

Mrs. September smiled, "Take a left, then a right, it's on your right-the corner class. Now off you go now, and no dillydallying!"

"Thank you very much, I'm Brandon Snow," I said as I backed away down the hall.

"I know!" She said as the elevator doors closed.

Oh wow, how? That was very strange and weird. How did Mrs. September know my name?

I really did not have time to ponder or think about that. I rushed left, then right, and then to the science classroom.

When I finally flung open the door, the class was already in session, and guess who do you think was sitting right in the front row, left center?

Yup, the girl who in all her glory - thanks for helping the new boy, I thought.

She smirked as I, Brandon, sank in the nearest seat.

CHAPTER FIVE

"V-I-O-L-A"

Genuine maturity and effectiveness hinge upon your heart and your relationship with your personal, spiritual well-being. When you understand this truth, your whole paradigm shifts.

This puts all Christians on the same level, from the high-profile ministers to the quietest members of the church. You have to be mindful of the heart of spiritual maturity to be transformed in your everyday faith walk!

Ever since Ben Zimmer, who used to be one of our chamber music ensemble members, moved, we have been looking for a new *"viola"* player. This has been going on for the last several months.

Ben was an awesome viola player. He also was one of our founding chamber music group members. I, Brandon, know it sounds very corny, but that is how our little chamber music group feels. We meaning Ben, Masato, and I, Brandon, were the original trio, and we really took big pride in our personal accomplishment of being in the chamber music group. Not that we are bragging, but playing classical music requires very, very, very good discipline and you do have to have good ethics, and most of all team spirit.

Sometimes you think your school day and life will be smooth sailing, only to discover things do not always happen as you thought – who would ever have thought that replacing Ben – our fabulous *viola* player – would be very difficult.

Yes,

Who would ever have thought that looking for a *viola* instrument player was like looking for a needle in a hay-stack.

But I, Brandon, and Masato promised to the chamber music ensemble that we both will continue to search and are forever looking.

One morning during a relaxing mindful experience, I was leading myself and was reflecting and praying – please, help our chamber music club find a *viola* player.

As I, Brandon, was reading my piano music and poetry book to get inspired, I hoped to find time out, a sense of peace, and an opportunity to experience relaxation and breathing – not to get overly stressed out. Searching for the *viola* player created a lot more stress than I ever imagined.

Whenever I was having trouble with something, I thought maybe my Mom would have a solution – therefore I went to the Rose Café.

When Brandon first walked inside the Rose-Café, his mother greeted him. As Brandon was looking around the café – his mother smiled from behind the counter and greeted Brandon, "Oh, hello Brandon, what brings you to the café at this time of the day? Is everything okay?" As Brandon was sitting on a stool and was looking at his mom, "No – nothing is really wrong – except Masato and I are having a very hard time looking for our new "*viola*" player for our quaint chamber music group."

Brandon was thinking to himself – this *viola* thing is really giving me a big-big-big-big major headache. He didn't realize that he was talking aloud to himself – his mother tells him, "Brandon – turn around and look toward the window seat at the end, what do you see?" As Brandon was slowly turning the stool seat and slowly turning toward the window booth, he noticed this girl who was sitting by herself and reading a Louis L'Amour book. He also noticed a music book. It looked as though the music book looked like it had either piano or *viola* music sheets in it.

He was thinking to himself: should I go and check it out – or just sit where I am. After a few minutes, he got some courage and decided to walk over toward where this girl was sitting – maybe it was a *viola* or a piano book, he wasn't sure. He thought to himself: yes, our chamber group is really desperate – I really don't have anything to lose.

As Brandon was walking toward where this girl was sitting, he was thinking this is really dumb – why am I doing this – what if I totally make a fool of myself – well too-late – the next thing he saw was this girl looking at me - with her big blue eyes and a very nice smile.

She said "Hi!" Brandon smiled back and was looking at the music book on the table – "Y-E-S," it is a *viola* music book. He was so excited. He asked her, "Do you play the *viola*?"

The girl smile and replied, "Yes I do, and my name is Brooke Donskoi."

CHAPTER SIX

MR. SATO

On Wednesday after school, Brandon was sitting at the kitchen table and looking at Lake Minihaha, and was just thinking - not anything special was going on. His Dad came to stand next to where Brandon was sitting. Brandon greeted his Dad – "Hi Dad, I was not aware that you were home!"

His father replied, "Yes, I canceled my patients for this afternoon," as he was looking at Brandon with something on his mind.

His Dad was looking out the kitchen window, which overlooks Lake Minihaha, and after awhile with a deep sigh – "Brandon, I have something to tell you." Then with another deep sigh....

"Brandon, this morning I received a telephone call telling me that your former piano teacher Mr. Paul Ross had died. I know how much you really liked Mr. Ross, and how fond you were of him. I also know how much Mr. Ross cared for you. I just wanted to tell you how very much I'm sorry to tell you this bad news."

After that, his dad touched Brandon's shoulder and left the kitchen.

Brandon was thinking to himself about how much he enjoyed having Mr. Ross as his first piano teacher – he was always very patient – always was very kind – always was very understanding.

Mr. Ross always made piano playing fun for me. He always had a big smile when Brandon first walked inside of Mr. Ross's old, white, single-story house, with a white picket fence.

I, Brandon, could still remember how Mr. Ross always encouraged and motivated me to learn each piano lesson in a fun way.

Even though I was only to have a piano lesson for forty-five minutes, somehow, Mr. Ross always found at least one hour to sometimes two hours for me. He would always tell me that I need to go home and practice piano. Even though I sometimes knew that I really did not need to practice piano, I always did and listened to what Mr. Ross told me to do.

As Brandon was looking at Lake Minihaha, all the emotion just crept up on him and he started to cry. He was thinking about how Mr. Ross told him one piano lesson day, "Brandon, I think there are a lot of other composers other than Ludwig van Beethoven."

With this thought, Brandon smiled.

After the news that Mr. Ross is no longer around this world, Brandon just couldn't practice piano Thursday and Friday. Here it is Saturday morning and he has to go to his piano lesson, but nothing is working for him.

That Saturday morning, Brandon went to his piano lesson at Mr. Sato's house.

Mr. Sato greeted Brandon at the front door. Brandon nodded to his piano teacher with a lukewarm smile, not his usual big, happy smile.

This week he was working on learning Sonata Op. 101 by Beethoven. As Brandon sat down in front of the piano, he started to play the music on the piano. All of the emotion inside of him immediately just came out and he started to cry.

Mr. Sato understood Brandon. He touched Brandon's hand and asked Brandon, "Did something happen?"

Brandon told Mr. Sato about Mr. Paul Ross and the news that Mr. Paul Ross passed away. Mr. Sato told Brandon, "Let's stop the piano lesson today. I have something to tell you, Brandon, someone once told me that life is not an easy life. It can get windy and rainy when flowers start to bloom. If this happens, then that life is full of goodbyes. Either you can accept what happens to yourself and others or not.

For something in life, don't dwell on yourself. Instead use that gift and energy to do the things that you are gifted and blessed with - that you can do."

After Brandon heard what Mr. Sato told him, Brandon looked at Mr. Sato and smiled.

Mr. Sato continued, "I'm very sorry to hear of Mr. Ross's passing. I was told he was a great man and a great piano teacher. Your Dad telephoned me

Wednesday." Brandon replied and told Mr. Sato, "Yes, he was a great person and a great piano teacher."

Mr. Sato told Brandon, "I know what you are saying – I once had a great teacher and when my piano teacher passed, my new piano teacher understood how I felt."

Brandon told Mr. Sato, "Thank you very much for the conversation and the words of wisdom - and for understanding.

Thank you for stopping the piano lesson. I will never forget the words of wisdom."

CHAPTER SEVEN

RANDOM ACTS OF KINDNESS

Words to live by.

Practice kindness – that is what my mom always tells Emily, George, and me, Brandon. Kindness is a virtue that stands out in a community where we live.

Sometimes there is a showing of harshness and selfishness.

Kindness is an attractive quality evident not only on our faces, but especially in our community when one is doing the right things to be kind to another person.

More importantly, kindness is an attribute that should characterize every believer because it is a reflection of goodness and blessings in us all.

Kindness is the outflow of goodness within.

Kindness is sometimes not seen as very important in our society. It is a very understandable trait of people who have faith and faithfulness. It includes being thoughtful in our approach to others, and not being focused on ourselves.

Kindness is being very sensitive to the needs of those around us and being ready to offer help with our words and actions.

We can learn to display kindness each day to others. These are the thoughts of my mom, Megan Snow.

Every Thursday, my mom closes the Rose Café after two p.m. to prepare hot meals for those in need.

The Rose-Café would open the doors at four thirty p.m. for the community outreach services and serve hot meals.

My mom and dad said they were very surprised at how many families who needed help came to our Rose Café for the hot meals.

CHAPTER EIGHT

A MESS OF THINGS

Sometimes when you think you're doing a good thing, it turns out to be a big mess of things.

Have you ever had days like that?

Even though you think you can manage to make it to all of your commitments, you plan ahead of your commitments - it turns out to be a total disaster – what a mess of things.

LATE AGAIN!

Matt Quiros – who is our flute player.

The fourth Saturday of each month – our chamber music club has a meeting and practice.

Peter, Masato, and I, Brandon, were there early.

Here it is one thirty p.m. and whoops!

Matt is not here again.

These past three meetings – Matt was coming to our chamber music club practices – late – and late – and late – again.

As quick as a flash, Matt opened his flute case – and donned a music sheet and music stand and was prepared to play – except he was playing the wrong music and the wrong tones.

As far as our chamber music club goes, we all did a little bit of everything. The four of us had been in the chamber music club and had been playing our respective musical instrument in the chamber music club for the last year now. Peter and Matt were added to our chamber music group after the founders Brandon, Masato, and Ben Zimmer, who is no longer with the group, founded the quaint little ensemble.

We knew each other very well and all of us acted as professional music players. We had gotten into a very comfortable and efficient rhythm of who did what.

Matt was thinking to himself.

"Here I am playing the wrong music and wrong notes on the flute – this is a total disaster – what a mess."

Finally, the quartet stopped playing.

I felt really bad about being late. I wanted to apologize, but I was way too scared to bring it up. Brandon, Masato, and Peter would be super mad.

I really did not like it when our little ensemble group of friends were mad at me. I really did not like that feeling more than any other feeling in the whole wide world.

I could hear the harsh sound of Masato, who said to me – "Matthew, today must be your lucky day."

I thought to myself – "What's lucky about being late?" Also, Masato called my full name – I could only think when my mother was upset with me, usually she would call-out my full name.

I knew it was better to just say it than to try to pretend it didn't happen.

"You're lucky because you only have two notes to play tomorrow," Brandon explained. His voice was a lot less tense, "Yeah," said Peter. Peter continued, "You are lucky and you will get away with it, again."

The awfully bad feeling in my stomach grew worse. I really wasn't trying to get away with anything.

After a deep sigh, I told the group, "Thanks for understanding that I was late, you guys are the best.

I really do have a good excuse!

My basketball game yesterday got cancelled because of some unforeseeable water leak and it was rescheduled for this morning. The game was 49-49, and we went into overtime….."

Brandon sighed and put his music sheet into his backpack, "That's the problem, Matthew – you always have an excellent – good excuse."

I replied, "Since when is having a good to excellent excuse a bad thing?"

I tried a half-smile and tried to bring a little sunny-side-up – a little cheerfulness to the whole pickle situation.

Brandon glanced at Masato and Peter – they seemed to have an entire conversation with their face expression in mere seconds. It seemed like an eternity, even though it was only a few seconds.

Peter said, "Look Matt I'm here to tell you that I'm waiting for the day when you tell somebody that the reason you need to leave early is because you have a responsibility to be at your job with our chamber music group."

Peter continued: "Besides, Mr. Sato pays you for being in the chamber music group."

Peter continued: "Why is everything else more important to you than being here to practice with our music group?"

Matt said, "Really, I love our chamber music group... you know that. I'm just... well... I guess I'm just so used to being late that it isn't really that late to me. Anyway, I just thought you or you guys would understand."

"We all do understand – you're really taking advantage of your friendships," Masato said.

"It really is not cool Matthew," said Peter.

Oh boy, this is not a good direction I thought, another ouch. This day was just not getting any better... as a matter of fact it was getting worse and worse.

Yes, organizing a chamber music club's practices was my choice and I do have to admit I have to own up to it.

I needed to take it just as seriously as basketball, student council, and all of the other things I did.

They were all commitments I made and even more importantly, they were all so much fun. That's why I committed to do so many things in the first place.

I love music, meeting new people, and being involved in lots of stuff and activity.

Sometimes it did make my head spin, but in a super good, fun, and excited way.

I liked being on the go, go, go, go, go!

In many ways, Brandon is very calm and is a structured guy.

Masato is very efficient and is a precise girl.

Peter, I really don't know too much about him.... Other than... he is always on time for our chamber music group practices.

Matt said, "Listen, you guys, I am really, really, really truly, truly, truly very, very, very, very sorry. Okay? I will really try hard to make our chamber music group practice meeting five minutes early!"

Peter, Masato, and Brandon sighed.

All in unison, "We know, Matt. It's just that you have said that before."

Brandon smiled and was studying Matt when Brandon said, "Let's patch up. Friends.

Best friends.

We are all best friends in the whole world."

"Thanks Brandon," Matt said. "I am very relieved to have been forgiven. I really mean it."

"You're welcome," said Brandon.

Brandon continued: "Just don't abuse the forgiveness of your late habit, okay?"

"Yeah," Masato agreed.

"Promise us you won't add any more things to your schedule, Matthew.

You can't handle it, and we meaning Brandon, Peter, and I, Masato, can't either; got it?"

Matt nodded vigorously, "I promise I won't! I swear and wholeheartedly promise."

The four of us linked and did *hi fives*, and just like that, the day was as fresh as sunshine.

On the way out, Brandon made an announcement:

"Viola player found."

CHAPTER NINE

GEORGE SNOW: JUNIOR RUGBY GUY

The rugby academies of Scotland are open to the best talent – eligible people are males from the age of fourteen onwards.

My big brother George happens to be a super, awesome, talented rugby player.

Yesterday, George got a letter of acceptance from the Scottish rugby academy.

This is a national academy structure designed to give young rugby stars a pathway into the professional leagues.

Meet George Snow, the American taking on Scotland's top rugby league.

For a talented young player in Scotland, the path to making it in this game is pretty well there for you.

From school and junior clubs to academies - usually you are making the pro-side in three major leagues as so many of these athletes thunder along it. That is George's goal.

CHAPTER TEN

ALMOST THERE

Several days ago, my older brother George, who is in tenth grade, got a letter of acceptance from the Scottish rugby academy. He was absolutely over the moon.

George will be leaving for Scotland for the next six months and will be working on training his technique and skills. George of course will be engaging his school academics.

Even though George is not very smart in academics, he really doesn't care. He got accepted into the Scottish super league junior program at the academy.

The league only accepted twenty potential rugby players.

Naturally, George was feeling enthusiastic about going to Scotland.

I, Brandon, felt optimistic about everything. George will be fine.

After all, this is what George always wanted - becoming a professional rugby player.

In fact, George has been going to a rugby summer youth program for seven weeks each of the last five years.

George is hoping to be a great rugby player, like our Dad was before retiring.

Our Dad, Mike, was a great rugby player when he was young.

Now he is a great dentist.

Our Dad played rugby for four teams for a total of seventeen seasons.

He will go down as one of the most clutch performers of his generation, a distinction he cemented with his first post-season appearance when he was only nineteen years old.

He was named "man of the match," six times during his time in the final cup games.

My Dad became a quiet leader, offering advice and pointers. His teammates respected him, knowing not only his on-field success, but also his good work ethic and time doing community service.

He was especially involved and helped tremendously when some rugby players had depression and alcohol abuse problems.

Many players often told others that Mike is very outstanding. There's something about his voice; he doesn't talk much, but when he does talk you want to listen.

Some remarked that he's got a lot of good input. It's nice to have one of those voices that's been around for a while - said some of teammates from some of his seventeen seasons.

After playing rugby for seventeen seasons, my Dad retired and became a dentist.

Now George is ready to become a rugby player.

Who knows how many years he might play.

Hopefully George will be a rugby guy, like our Dad.

Emily and Brandon are cheering for George's *success*.

Goodbye for now.

Goodbye for now.

Sequel coming soon.

Thank you very much for reading this book.

About the Author

Kevin graduated from Stanford University with a Bachelors of Science degree in Chemistry.

Kevin was a spelling bee winner, advancing to Washington, D.C., in fifth grade.

He also was an award-winning pianist in high school and at Stanford University.

His first book was titled *Sixth Grade and Growing Up*, and his second book was titled *Green Family: New Home* which is the first book in the series.

His mother considers him to be a great success.

All of his books can be found ---

on Amazon.com.

Made in the USA
Las Vegas, NV
25 July 2022

52147955R00031